SERIOUSLY SILLY

SCARY
FAIRY TALES

JACK and the
GIANT SPIDERWEB

Laurence Anholt
& Arthur Robins

ORCHARD

www.anholt.co.uk

GOOD EVENING, LADIES AND GENTLEMEN.

My name is
THE MAN WITHOUT A HEAD.

Of course, I have a head really...it's just that it is right here in my hands. It makes it so much easier to brush my teeth.

So, you like SCARY STORIES, do you?

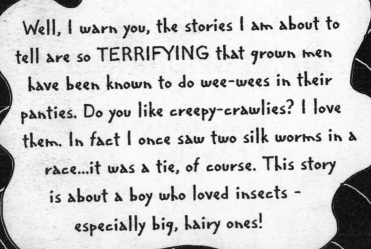

Well, I warn you, the stories I am about to tell are so TERRIFYING that grown men have been known to do wee-wees in their panties. Do you like creepy-crawlies? I love them. In fact I once saw two silk worms in a race...it was a tie, of course. This story is about a boy who loved insects - especially big, hairy ones!

There was once a funny boy named Jack who lived in a tiny house with his Aunt Grimewiper.

SERIOUSLY SILLY

SCARY
FAIRY TALES

JACK and the
GIANT SPIDERWEB

ORCHARD BOOKS
338 Euston Road, London NW1 3BH
Orchard Books Australia
Level 17/207 Kent Street, Sydney, NSW 2000

First published in 2014 by Orchard Books
ISBN 978 1 40832 957 3

A CIP catalogue record for this book is available
from the British Library.

1 3 5 7 9 10 8 6 4 2

Printed and bound by CPI Group (UK) Ltd, Croydon, CR0 4YY

Orchard Books is a division of Hachette Children's Books,
an Hachette UK company.

www.hachette.co.uk

Jack and Aunt Grimewiper were very poor, but the house was spotlessly clean. This was because Aunt Grimewiper spent every minute polishing and scrubbing.

If Aunt Grimewiper saw even a fly or a teeny flea, she would scream, "Eeeeek! Fly away, flea! Flee away, fly!"

If there was one thing she hated, it was messy boys. And if there was one thing she hated even more than messy boys, it was spiders in the bathtub.

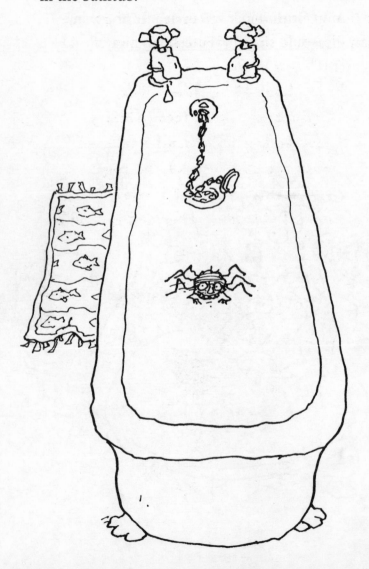

It was a shame that Aunt Grimewiper hated insects so much, because Jack loved them! Butterflies, bluebottles, beetles, millipedes, maggots, moths – Jack loved them all. He liked insects so much that he often danced about in a stripy bug suit, singing a little bug song.

"Look at me, I'm a bee,
Buzzing like a teeny flea.
I love to hug the worms and bugs,
Kiss the spiders and the slugs.
Insects are what I enjoy,
They call me Jack, Hug-a-Bug boy!"

Jack was kind to every creepy-crawly, but his favourite pet was a huge, hairy spider called Webster. Jack spent all his time playing with him. He made Webster a spider playground and a little spider boat to float next to him in the bath, and even a spider sleeping bag out of a pencil case.

"Goodnight, Webster, you lovely, hairy spider," he would whisper.

Of course, Jack had to hide Webster from Aunt Grimewiper. He could always tell when she had found him, because Aunt Grimewiper would leap on a chair and scream, "EEEEEEK! There's that hideous, horrible, hairy spider."

Then she would chase Webster all over the house with her broom.

"If only you were a clever boy," said Aunt Grimewiper, "you would think of a way of making money, instead of playing with creepy-crawlies."

"I am a clever boy," said Jack. "Look, I have invented a spider bicycle with eight little pedals."

Then Aunt Grimewiper chased Jack and
Webster all over the house with her broom.

One day, Aunt Grimewiper opened the kitchen cupboard and there was nothing to eat at all.

"All I want is one little egg for my tea," she wailed. "Wait...I have an idea! Why don't you take that horrible spider to the pet shop and see if you can sell him?"

Jack was very sad to say goodbye to Webster, but he wanted to please his aunt. So he put Webster on top of his bug hat and set off to buy an egg for Aunt Grimewiper.

On the way, he met a strange old man hunting for insects with a net.

"That's a fine looking spider, sonny," said the strange old man. "I would like to buy him from you."

"What will you give me?" said Jack.

"Hmm..." said the strange old man. "How about a little egg?"

Jack remembered how much Aunt Grimewiper had wanted a little egg for her tea. So he agreed.

With tears in his eyes, Jack kissed his spider goodbye. The man put Webster carefully in a box, then he reached out and gave Jack something in return.

Jack stared into his hand. "I can't see an egg!" he said.

"Look carefully," said the strange old man. "It's a spider's egg. Spiders' eggs are tiny. And what's more – this is a MAGIC SPIDER'S EGG!"

Jack looked again. There was an egg there. It was as small as a grain of sand.

He took the egg carefully back to the
house where he found Aunt Grimewiper cleaning
the bathtub.

"Look!" said Jack proudly. "I have brought you a
little egg."

"Oh, Jack!" groaned Aunt Grimewiper. "This
egg isn't big enough to feed a flea."

Then Aunt Grimewiper took the tiny egg and
washed it down the plughole.

Jack went sadly to bed – Webster was gone and there wasn't even an egg for tea.

He was just dropping off to sleep when he heard a loud noise from the bathroom. "EEEEEEEEEEEEEK!!" screamed Aunt Grimewiper. "A HUGE, HORRIBLE, HAIRY SPIDER!!!"

Jack hopped out of bed and ran into the bathroom. There was Aunt Grimewiper in her dressing gown, standing on a stool. She was trembling from head to foot and pointing at the bathtub with her broom.

Jack looked in the bathtub. He saw a huge, red face with eight scary eyes. It was a spider...but this spider was as big as a balloon! It was the biggest spider Jack had ever seen.

Now if you saw a spider as big as a balloon, I
expect you would SCREAM and run and tell a
policeman, then the policeman would SCREAM
too. But as I have told you – Jack loved spiders.

"Oh look, Aunt Grimewiper," he said. "Isn't he
lovely? He's even bigger than Webster."

But Aunt Grimewiper had picked up her broom and she was just about to wallop the spider, when WHOOSH! The enormous spider hopped out of the tub, scuttled across the floor, and tied Aunt Grimewiper tightly in a web.

Aunt Grimewiper tried to scream, but she was wrapped as neatly as a Christmas present. The spider strapped her on his back and clambered out of the bathroom window.

Jack didn't know what to do. He found a torch and ran into the moonlit garden.

He couldn't believe his eyes – a huge spider's web stretched higher than the roof of the house, far into the starry sky. It was glistening with tiny dewdrops like a million diamonds. It was the most beautiful thing Jack had ever seen.

And high above his head was the huge red spider, with Aunt Grimewiper strapped on its back. So what did Jack do? He took the web firmly in his hands, and he began to climb.

And on the way, he sang a little song.

"Incy Wincy spider,
Big as a balloon,
Climb a giant spider's web
Halfway to the moon."

Jack climbed higher than his house, higher than the trees, but he couldn't catch the spider. He looked down at the countryside far below, and there was their house, as small as a sugar cube.

Up he went, as high as the starry sky. At last, Jack reached the top of the spiderweb, just in time to see the huge, red spider scuttling off into the clouds – and now the spider was as big as a horse!

Jack looked around. He was amazed to find himself standing in a magical landscape, filled with giant insects of every kind. "Oh!" gasped Jack in delight. "Big Bug Land."

Jack ran about hugging all the bugs he could find. There were ants as big as elephants and snails as big as sheds. He saw cockroaches as big as cars, and bees as big as buses. Above Jack's head flew dragonflies and butterflies as big as planes.

He jumped out of the way just in time, as a centipede as long as a train came rushing by.

Jack searched everywhere, but he couldn't see the giant red spider or Aunt Grimewiper.

Suddenly a fly as big as a helicopter landed beside him and began to wash her hands.

"Excuse me," said Jack nervously. "Have you seen a giant red spider with a little lady on his back?"

The huge fly pointed with one long leg. In the distance, Jack could see Aunt Grimewiper and the giant red spider scuttling up a hill.

"Oh no!" said Jack sadly. "I'll never catch them."

The huge bluebottle looked kindly at Jack and lifted him gently onto her back. Then she flapped her huge, transparent wings and they were off – over the countryside and into the hills. Every now and then, Jack saw the huge spider below. Each time he saw it, the spider seemed to have grown.

At the top of the hill was a huge spider cave. The bluebottle landed gently beside it. Jack climbed down and patted her head. "Thank you, fly," he said.

Jack pulled his torch out of his pocket, and shone it into the dark cave. He saw eight eyes as big as swimming pools. And they were all staring at him.

Now, if you saw a spider with eyes as big as swimming pools, I expect you would SCREAM and SCREAM until you were sick. But, as I keep telling you, Jack adored spiders.

He crept into the dark cave. And on the way, he sang a little song.

"Incy Wincy spider,
With legs as long as trees,
Your eyes are big as swimming pools,
Can I come in, please?"

There was the massive red spider, bigger than a house. And there was Aunt Grimewiper, dangling upside down from the ceiling. The spider looked at her hungrily, and span her round and round. Then in a huge voice, the spider said,

"Fum, Fo, Fee, Fi,
I think I've caught a tasty fly!"

"Oh, please," said Jack. "That's not a fly. That's Aunt Grimewiper."

"Fum, Fo, Fi, Fee,
I think I'll eat her for my tea."

"Wait," said Jack. "I'll show you my insect dance." Then Jack buzzed round and round in his bug suit and sang his little bug song.

> "Look at me, I'm a bee,
> Buzzing like a teeny flea.
> I love to hug the worms and bugs,
> Kiss the spiders and the slugs.
> Insects are what I enjoy,
> They call me Jack, Hug-a-Bug boy!"

The spider thought about this for a moment. Then he gave Jack a huge hairy hug and carefully unwrapped Aunt Grimewiper. She was so grateful to Jack and the spider, that she cleaned up the spider's cave and left everything nice and tidy.

And because Jack had always been kind to creepy-crawlies, the spider said,

"Fee, Fi, Fum, Fo,
Here's a present before you go!"

He walked to the other side of his cave and came back with a huge shiny gold coin.

"Of course!" laughed Jack. "You're a money spider!"

"Oh, Jack! You are a clever boy," said Aunt Grimewiper proudly.

Then Jack said goodbye to the huge money spider. He took Aunt Grimewiper by the hand and rolled his gold coin down the hill and all the way through the creepy-crawly world.

When he found the giant spiderweb, he tied the coin on his back, and Jack and Aunt Grimewiper climbed down, down, down all the way to their little house.

Jack went straight to town and put the big gold coin in the bank. Then he bought lots of lovely things for Aunt Grimewiper to eat and a shiny new vacuum cleaner for a present. He was just coming home, when he met the strange man sitting on the garden wall, with Webster in a jam jar.

So, Jack bought Webster back from the strange man. Webster was very pleased to see Jack again. And Jack was very pleased to see Webster.

Then Jack, Aunt Grimewiper, Webster and the strange old man sat at the table and they ate the most delicious breakfast you have ever seen.

SERIOUSLY SILLY

SCARY
FAIRY TALES

LAURENCE ANHOLT & ARTHUR ROBINS

COLLECT THEM ALL!

Also available as an ebook